說好話，好好說，誰先說

文／孟瑛如
圖／梁雯媛
英文翻譯／吳侑達

兔寶寶阿立閃著兩顆大門牙，頭搖得像波浪鼓似的一直說：「不要，不要，我討厭……」

「不要，不要，我就是不要！」
隨即張大嘴巴、露出大門牙，開始
不停的尖叫！

「不要！」是阿立最
近學會的兩個字，尖叫
是他的最新武器，

只要兩者並用，就算理
不直氣不壯，也能嚇到
所有人，這樣阿立就能
得到他想要的東西。

因此，阿立每天都
會使用他的新武器來
得到想要的東西，

一天還會用上很多
次呢！

有一次，阿立因為尖叫過度
而岔了氣，連額頭上的毛都豎
直了。

他看到自己在鏡子裡的這副
模樣，也不禁嚇了一大跳！

一開始，阿立使用「不要！」或「我討厭……」加上尖叫的新武器時，兔媽媽都會急著一把抱住他，溫柔的摸摸他那因哭得太用力而豎直的長耳朵說：

「怎麼啦？好好說。」
「說好話，好好說。」
「好好說，媽媽才知道你怎麼了。」

但一次、兩次……
很多次之後，

兔媽媽逐漸失去耐心，
也開始學起阿立使用「不要！」
或「我討厭……」加上尖叫的武器。

後來，只要阿立一說「不要！」或「我討厭……」，兔媽媽也會跟著豎直耳朵、露出比阿立更大的門牙、用更大的聲音怒吼回去：

「你再說不要或我討厭，我就不理你了！」

「你再說不要或我討厭，就回自己房間不要出來了！」

「你再說不要或我討厭，我今天晚上就不要講故事給你聽了！」

阿立其實也不想表現得這麼糟，更不希望兔媽媽不理他，但他覺得自己說也說不清，而且新武器好像也快沒有用了，不知道該怎麼辦才好。

媽媽真的不理阿立了！

阿立開始覺得好寂寞……

已經好久沒有看到媽媽的笑容了——

現在的媽媽總是露出大門牙、豎直耳朵，板著一張說不出有
多生氣的臉！

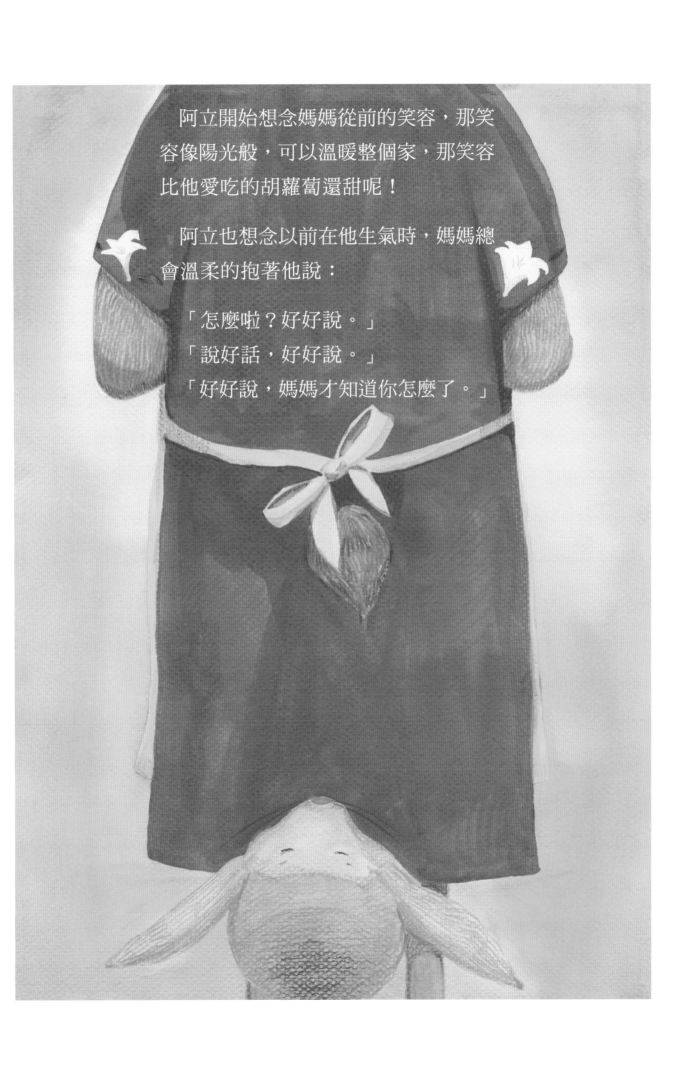

阿立開始想念媽媽從前的笑容，那笑
容像陽光般，可以溫暖整個家，那笑容
比他愛吃的胡蘿蔔還甜呢！

阿立也想念以前在他生氣時，媽媽總
會溫柔的抱著他說：

「怎麼啦？好好說。」
「說好話，好好說。」
「好好說，媽媽才知道你怎麼了。」

這天早上，阿立又將玩過的玩具、看完的繪本丟了一地，媽媽正要清理地板，便催促阿立說：「趕快收好，我要拖地！」

阿立也習慣性的說：「不要！我討厭收東西！」

兔媽媽就立刻大聲吼叫：「叫你收拾就收拾！不然我就要把你的東西全部丟掉！沒看過這麼不聽話的孩子！」

這時候，阿立想到媽媽過去常說的話，於是脫口而出：

「媽媽，妳不是常說要好好說，說好話嗎？」

「要好好說，說好話。媽媽，為什麼妳不先說？」

兔媽媽愣了一下，接著輕聲的說：「媽媽要拖地了，我們一起收拾吧。」

　　阿立也好好的回答：「我再玩一下就會自己收拾了。」

隔天一早，兔媽媽說：「起床吃早餐囉！」

阿立又習慣性的說：「我不要……」

這時候，兔媽媽溫柔的說：「有你愛吃的吐司夾胡蘿蔔炒蛋喔！要趁熱吃才好吃！」

　　阿立發現媽媽變得不一樣了，趕緊說：「真的嗎？那我先刷牙再來吃！」

吃完早餐，阿立蹦蹦跳跳的要跑到外面玩，兔媽媽又習慣性的大叫：「別亂跑，待會兒你會跌倒！」

　　說完，兔媽媽自己愣了一下，接著改口說：「在院子裡玩就好，院子外面的馬路車子多，比較危險。」

阿立問媽媽：「媽媽，什麼是『說好話』呢？」

兔媽媽說：「就是把話說好，把話說對！」

阿立繼續問：「『好好說』又是什麼意思呢？」

兔媽媽回答：「就是說出你要如何做，說出怎樣才能夠做得到。」

阿立再問：「那麼，『誰先說』呢？」

兔媽媽立刻露出大門牙，笑得很甜蜜的說：「誰先想到誰先說啊！想到就可以立刻說。」

於是，兔媽媽摟著阿立，燦爛的笑著說：「我們可以一起好好說，一起說好話！」

　　繪本中兔寶寶阿立和兔媽媽的故事，是很多父母在教養子女過程中經常會面對的情況。我們都知道對待孩子要正向支持，要說好話、說對的話，而且要好好說，但應該由誰先說呢？

　　在親子相處的過程中，我們常會忘了「情感贊同，價值中立」的說話方式，忘了是要讓孩子學會和我們做討論，而不是談論或辯論，最後因情緒管理問題，流於互相指責對方不說好話，然後說出更多不知所云的壞話。話說出口只是瞬間，遺忘卻需要很久，壞話會變成不好的記憶，要花許久才能遺忘，許多孩子可以面對事實，卻沒辦法面對可能是善意的壞話。我們尤其建議父母或師長不要自己找藉口，認為是出於善意，就可以任意說話，例如：擔心對方會遭遇不好的事就先預告不幸，而非幫忙解決或是善意提醒如何做。如同文中兔寶寶阿立要到外面玩，兔媽媽一開始說的是：「別再亂跑，待會兒你會跌倒！」其實可以換成這麼說：「在院子裡玩就好，院子外面的馬路車子多，比較危險。」

　　2010 年時我曾在心理出版社出版了《不要比較，只要教我：親職教育貼心手冊》，書中針對父母或師長在教養過程中如何對孩子下指令，做了以下四大步驟的描述：（1）說出你打算要做的，這意謂著你自己必須非常清楚的定義出相關的規定、限制和期望；（2）做到你所說的，當你設立一項規定或是表達出你的期望時，你必須非常肯定，一旦說出就要做到，所以說之前必須考慮情境、執行的可能及自己的可監督性，因唯有事情是可行的、能監督孩子的行為，以確保他確實去做了，才有達成目標的可能；（3）確定你的要求是一致的，你必須對你所說的和你打算要做的決定，保持堅決肯定和一致的態度，因為在教養上的法則是：一旦你曾經破例，孩子總是永遠記得；（4）讓孩子為自己的行為負責，告訴孩子你打算怎麼做，讓他相信你是勢在必行的，給你自己足夠的權力與堅持度，成為一個言行一致並且能給予孩子期望的父母。

　　父母都期待自己能成為好父母，師長也期待自己是好師長，孩子更希望自己是好孩子，若每個人都有好的動機、好的期許，那就讓我們從好好說話、說好話開始。由自己先開始說，讓好話變成善意的提醒，讓好話變成每個人的幸福，不要再有難以抹滅、不幸的壞話記憶，因為幸福就是幸福，不幸才是故事。希望親子共讀完此繪本後，從此只有幸福，沒有故事。

Tell Me Nicely and Properly

Written by Ying-Ru Meng
Illustrated by Wen-Yuan Liang
Translated by Arik Wu

A Li the Baby Bunny, with his two upper incisor teeth showing, shook his head like a drum-shaped rattle, constantly saying the word "no" and the phrase "I don't like it"!

"No, no, no! I don't like it!" he screamed nonstop with his mouth wide open, showing even more of his incisor teeth.

"No" was the word he just recently learned, and screaming was his newest "weapon". The combination of the two could easily cow other people into letting him have his way, even when he was the one at fault!

Every single day, he used this trick to get what he wanted, and not just once, but multiple times.

One time A Li screamed so hard that he not only had a side stitch, but also had his hair standing straight as if there were static electricity. When he saw himself in the mirror, even he himself was frightened by what he had seen.

When A Li first began screaming "no" and "I don't like it" at the top of his lungs, his Mother would quickly hold him into her loving arms, gently patting his straightened ears. "What happened? Please tell me!" she said.

"Tell me 'nicely' and 'properly," she continued. "Or else Mommy won't know what happened."

Mama Rabbit gradually grew rather impatient, however, after having repeated this for a bit too many times. She now went with the same trick in response.

Mama Rabbit no longer patted A Li gently on the ears when he screamed "no" or "I don't like it", but straightened her rabbit ears, showed her larger upper incisor teeth, and yelled back even louder.

"If you keep saying 'no' or 'I don't like it', I'm not going to talk to you anymore."

"If you keep saying 'no' or 'I don't like it', I'd have to ask you to stay in your room for the rest of the day!"

"If you keep saying 'no' or 'I don't like it', I'm not going to read you stories tonight!"

In fact, A Li did not want to behave this badly, nor did he want Mommy to give him the cold shoulder, but he felt like he could never make himself clear and his new weapon was quickly losing its magic. He did not know what to do.

Mama Rabbit no longer talked to A Li...

A Li felt so lonely.

He had not seen Mommy's smile for a long time. Now all he saw every day was her angrily straightened ears, large threatening incisor teeth, and that infuriated face!

A Li started to miss the days when Mommy was all smiles with him. Mommy's smile was like sunshine - melting away the gloom in the family, and even sweeter than A Li's favorite carrots.

He also started to miss the days when Mommy would hold him into her arms, gently whispering to him, "Tell me what happened. Tell me 'nicely' and 'properly', all right?"

This morning, A Li again scattered toys and picture books all over the floor. Mama Rabbit was just about to mop the floor, so she hastened A Li to clean up the mess he made.

Out of habit, A Li screamed, "No! I don't like cleaning up!"

Mama Rabbit instantly yelled back, "Don't you talk back to me! If you fail to clean up this mess, I'll throw away every single thing of yours! Seriously, I've never seen so disobedient a kid like you!"

At that moment, A Li suddenly recalled the things Mama Rabbit used to say.

"Mom, didn't you always say we should talk to each other 'nicely' and 'properly'?" he said. "Talk to me nicely and properly! Mommy, why don't you set the example first?"

Mama Rabbit stopped, looking stunned for a moment, and then collected herself and said in a rather gentle tone of voice, "Hey, let's clean up this mess together. Mommy has to mop the floor later."

A Li replied, "Roger that! I'll clean it up later myself. I just need a bit more time here."

The next morning, Mama Rabbit called out to A Li to come have his breakfast.

Out of habit, A Li again replied, "No..."

Not waiting for him to finish the sentence, Mama Rabbit continued gently, "I've made you your favorite breakfast: a scrambled egg sandwich with carrots. Eat it while it's hot so it tastes better."

There was something different about Mama Rabbit today, and A Li could sense it. So he quickly replied, "Really? Just a moment please. I have to brush my teeth."

After breakfast, A Li hopped all the way to the front yard to play, and Mama Rabbit habitually called out to him, "Don't hop around like that! You'll trip yourself."

But she soon realized she may have sounded a bit too harsh, so, with a softer tone of voice, she said again, "Hey, just play in the yard, all right? There are cars out there on the street. It's too dangerous."

Curiously, A Li asked, "Mommy, what exactly is it to say things 'nicely'?"

Mama Rabbit said, "It means 'to say things the right way'!"

"What does it mean to say things properly then?" A Li raised another question.

Mama Rabbit replied, "It means 'to state clearly what you want to do, and how you want to do it."